If You Were My Baby

A Wildlife Lullaby

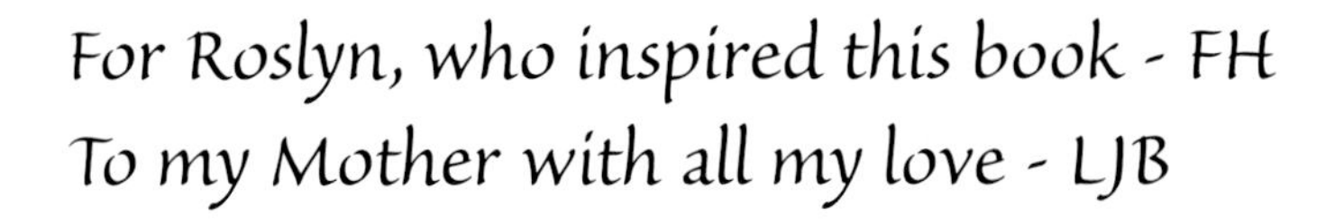

For Roslyn, who inspired this book - FH
To my Mother with all my love - LJB

A Sharing Nature With Children Book

Library of Congress Cataloging-in-Publication Data

Hodgkins, Fran, 1964-
If you were my baby : a wildlife lullaby / by Fran Hodgkins ; illustrated by Laura J. Bryant.-- 1st ed.
p. cm. -- (A sharing nature with children book)
Summary: At bedtime, a parent explains how animals, like humans, care for their young children and help them grow and thrive.
ISBN 1-58469-074-7 (hardback) -- ISBN 1-58469-075-5 (pbk.)
[1. Animals--Infancy--Fiction. 2. Parent and child--Fiction. 3. Bedtime--Fiction. 4. Animals--Fiction.] I. Bryant, Laura J., ill. II. Title. III. Series.
PZ7.H66475If 2005

2005005350

Dawn Publications
12402 Bitney Springs Road
Nevada City, CA 95959
530-274-7775
nature@dawnpub.com

Printed in China

10 9 8 7 6 5 4 3 2 1
First Edition

Design and computer production by Patty Arnold
Menagerie Design and Publishing

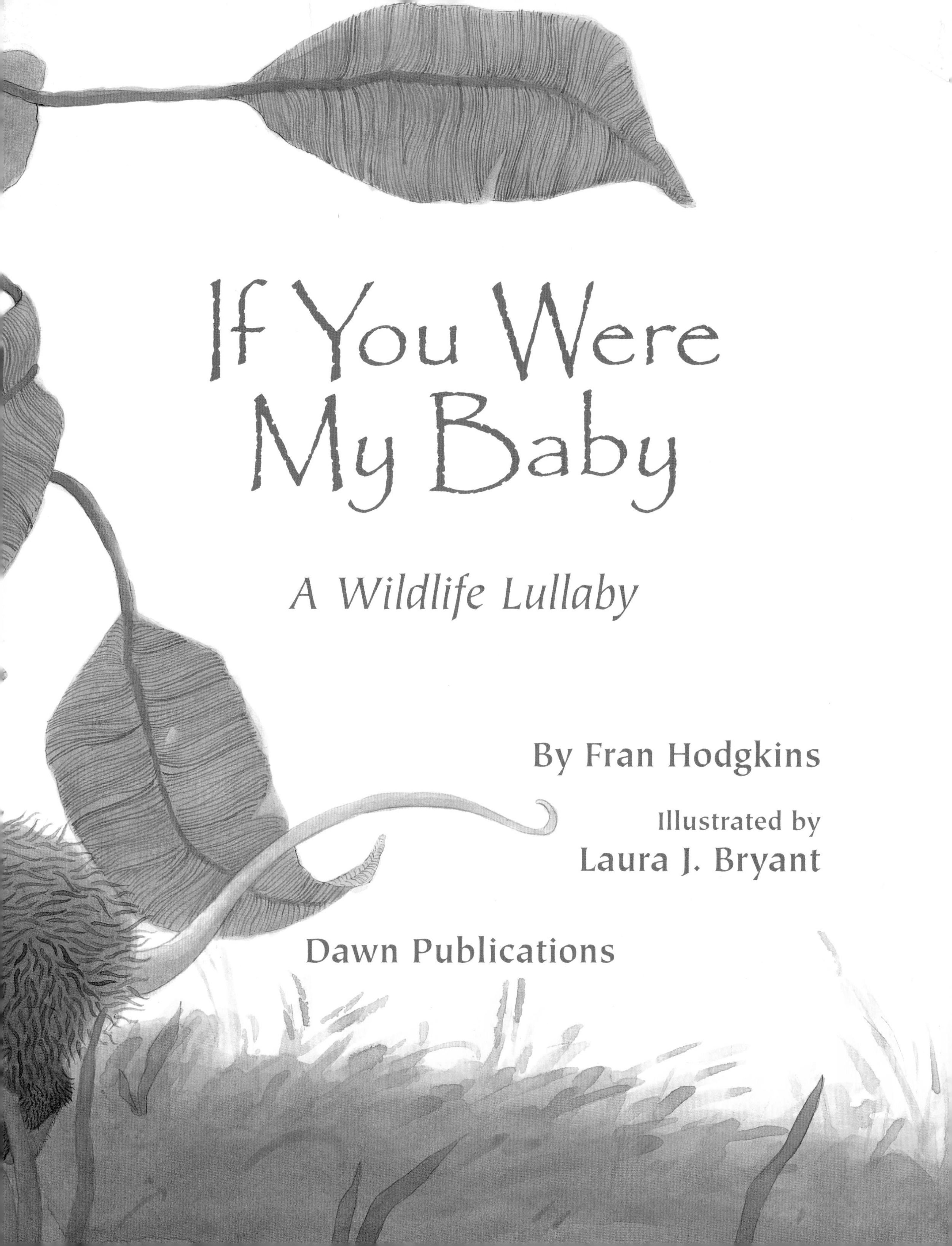

If You Were My Baby

A Wildlife Lullaby

By Fran Hodgkins

Illustrated by
Laura J. Bryant

Dawn Publications

If you were my baby squirrel,
I would welcome you to the world
In a secret nest I made just for you.

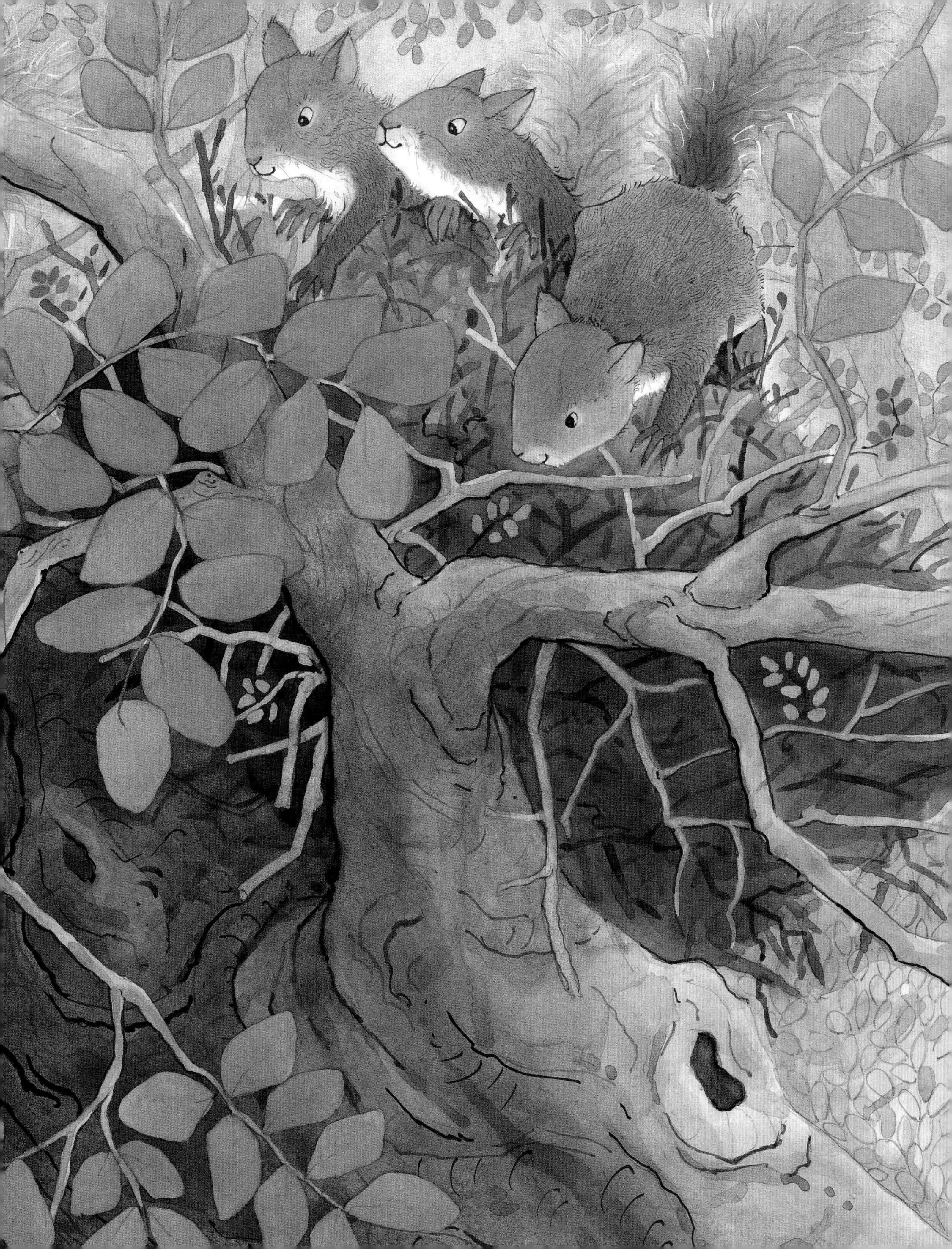

If you were my baby otter,
I would give you the sea for a playground
And rock you in the waves.

If you were my baby bear,
I would bring you out of winter's darkness
And into spring's warm light.

If you were my baby possum
I would carry you on my back
As you find your way in the world.

If you were my baby deer,
I would help you learn to step lightly
And find sweet flowers and tender grass.

If you were my baby duck,
I would paddle just ahead,
Leading you to the wonders of lakes and ponds.

If you were my baby bison,
I would watch as you explore the grassy prairie
And wait for you to come back to my side.

If you were my baby wolf,
I would teach you to sing to the stars,
Calling to your family, friends, and the whole world.

If you were my baby fox,
I would leap and run and tumble with you,
Helping you grow strong and smart.

If you were my baby beaver,
I would show you how to build well,
Using branches, mud, and hard work.

If you were my baby skunk,
I would teach you to have the patience
To give others fair warning before you act.

If you were my baby mountain goat,
I would gently lead you up the cliffs
To stand between Earth and sky.

If you were my baby bat,
I would soar with you below the stars
And hold you close when the night's flying is done.

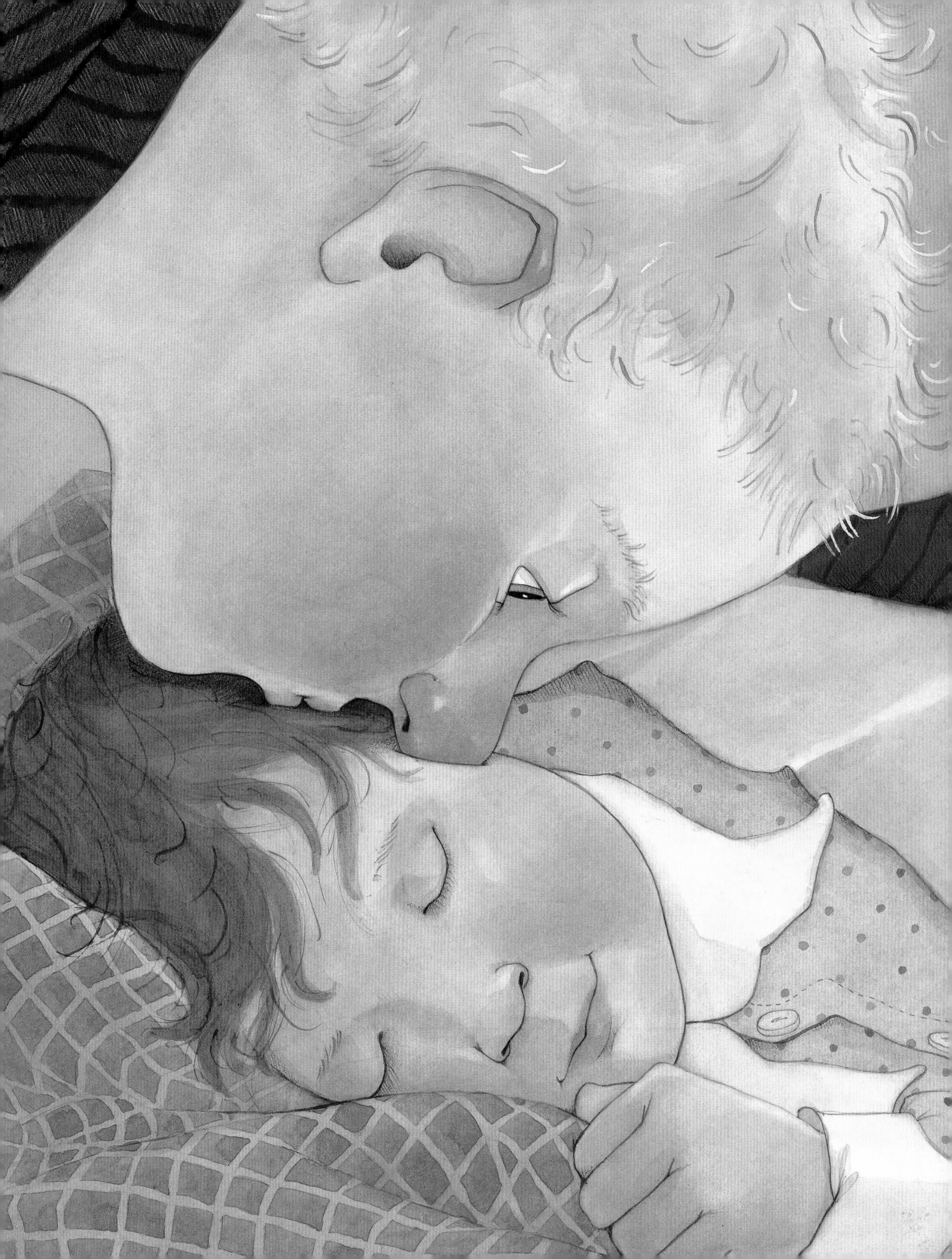

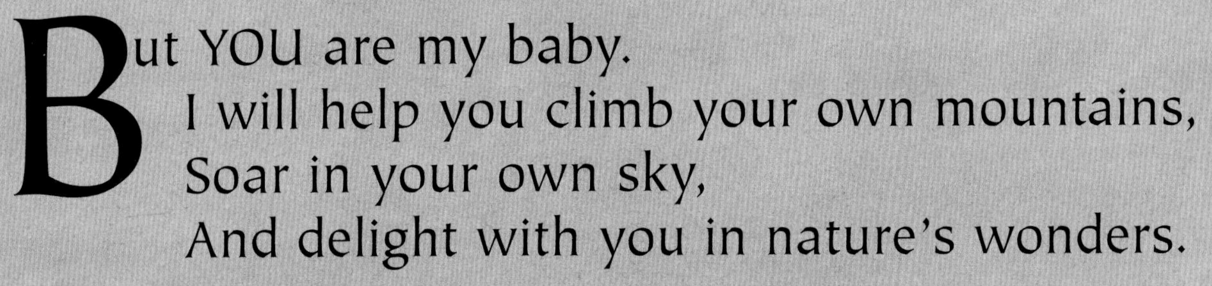

But YOU are my baby.
I will help you climb your own mountains,
Soar in your own sky,
And delight with you in nature's wonders.

But first, I'll tuck you in.

Photo © Black Inc. Digital

This book was inspired by at least three generations of women. Fran Hodgkins' mother taught her to love nature, and how to watch and "really see." An early memory of Fran's is watching for hours as a spider built a web on her tire swing. Now as a mother, Fran passes her love of wild things on to her daughter Rosie "without even really thinking about it." From their backyard in Lynn, Massachusetts, to the beach, to the forest, they watch. This book began with Rosie, and her questions about nature and animals.

Laura Bryant's studio is nestled in the Shenandoah Mountains of West Virginia. From her window, or nearby, she saw deer, fox, ducks, bats, possum, squirrels, skunks, and even a bear—all while she was illustrating this book! Laura is an award-winning children's book illustrator who loves to celebrate the beauty and intimacy of nature in her illustrations. Her hope is that the love and warmth between children and their parents is strengthened by their connection to the natural world around us.

A FEW OTHER NATURE AWARENESS BOOKS FROM DAWN PUBLICATIONS

Eliza and the Dragonfly by Susie Rinehart, illustrated by Anisa Claire Hovemann. This charming story revolves around the beauty and wonder of the hidden world that can be found in a local pond.

Forest Bright, Forest Night by Jennifer Ward, illustrated by Jamichael Henterly. Take a peek into the forest in the daytime, then flip the book to see the same forest at nighttime. Count the animals, and see who is asleep and who is busy!

All Around Me, I See by Laya Steinberg, illustrated by Cris Arbo. With eyes wide open to the wonders of nature, a child, tired from her hike, sleeps—and in her dream, flies like a bird and marvels at the life around her.

Earth Day, Birthday by Pattie Schnetzler, illustrated by Chad Wallace. To the tune of "The Twelve Days of Christmas," here is a sing-along, read-along book that honors the animals, the environment, and a universal holiday all in one fresh approach.

Sunshine On My Shoulders, Ancient Rhymes: A Dolphin Lullaby, and *Take Me Home, Country Roads,* all three books by John Denver and adapted and illustrated by Christopher Canyon. Stunningly beautiful, heartwarming books from the John Denver & Kids Series.

Dawn Publications is dedicated to inspiring in children a deeper understanding and appreciation for all life on Earth. To view our online catalog, visit www.dawnpub.com. Order online by calling 800-545-7475.